Hi I'm Feely and this is my diary.

There are six Feely books so far. It's best to read them in this order:

1    Feely's Magic Diary

2    Feely for Prime Minister

3    Feely and Her Well-Mad Parents

4    Feely Goes to Work

5    Feely and Henry VIII

6    Feely and Someone Else's Granny

Feely and her Well-Mad Parents
by Barbara Catchpole
Illustrated by Jan Dolby

Published by Ransom Publishing Ltd.
Unit 7, Brocklands Farm, West Meon, Hampshire GU32 1JN, UK
www.ransom.co.uk

ISBN      978 1785911231
First published in 2016

# Feely

## and her
## Well-Mad
## Parents

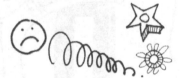

Barbara Catchpole

Illustrated by Jan Dolby

Ransom

# Monday

## Dear Diary

It's been a strange week! Just when you think everything's OK, it starts to come apart.

Life is like that. It's like when Nanna Tonks tried to teach me to knit. You take your eyes off it for one minute to watch Masterchef and there's a big knot. Before you know it, there's a hole and you have to make it into a scarf.

Perhaps I took that too far – but you know what I mean. Life is like knitting with a hole in it. Tricky!

I love my mum and dad to bits. I mean, if I am really famous now and you have bought my diary on ebay, I want you to know that I love my mum and dad to the moon and back.

But you must know that you can love someone and they can still send you raving, screaming, sobbing, yelling, barking bonkers! That's how families work.

My mum and dad don't talk to each other much. Here is an example. I'm going to underline it so you can see it properly.

ⓐⓜⓜⓜⓜ... .......

## The Example Starts Here

### My sports shirt with egg on it

My mum is a counsellor. That means she

helps sad people feel happy and
angry people feel calm.

She doesn't do that for me! Actually,
when I am calm she sometimes helps me to
feel really angry.

Last week I lost my sports shirt and
Miss Harty who does sports won't let you
sit it out. You have
to wear one from
Lost Property
and they are all
grey and manky
and far too big and
someone else has
sweated in it.

I hate Miss Harty. So I really needed to find it.

'Mum, where's my sports shirt?'

Mum!

'Where do *you* think it is, Feely?'

(See? You ask a question and instead of getting an answer, you get a question back! That's no way to get anything done. I wanted an answer, not another question!)

'I don't know.
I don't know where
my sports shirt is.
If I knew, I wouldn't
be asking you.
Instead I'd stuff it
in my sports bag
while I still stand

an ice lolly's chance in an oven of being on

time for school'

So I ask Dad.

Now Dad is a teacher, so he likes to tell

people stuff. Like you are eating pizza and

he has to tell you about Italy and volcanoes

and people being turned to stone. He can't

just let you eat
pizza in peace. He
goes on and on
until your teeth
fall out.

Anyway.

'Dad, where's my sports shirt?'

'Under the bed in Oliver's room, with egg
stains on it. Stuff it in your bag and get to
school before you're late.'

You see what I mean? Dad *knew* where
my shirt was all along. *And* he knew it was
dirty.

In any normal house, he would have told
Mum and she would have washed it and put

it in my sports bag. Piece of cake!

What happened was –
Oliver had a big zit on his
nose and I said he looked
like Rudolf. He flicked egg
at me and it got on the
wall in the kitchen that
Dad had just painted.

So I used the shirt to wipe the egg off
(most of it, anyway), then threw the shirt
at Oliver. Then Mum came in ('I can't leave
you two alone for a minute.')

It wasn't fair – it wasn't *me*, it was
him.

I don't know how my shirt got under

Ollie's bed. I can't keep track of everything!

That's what parents are for. It's their job!

That's what I'm saying: my parents are

rubbish. They just don't do their jobs.

## End of example

So it was kind of strange when Mum and

Dad started to act weird.

First, my mum never gets stressy. She is very calm and very slow and sort of happy. (Don't tell her, but it stresses me out just looking at her)

So there she was, in the middle of the living room in just her bra and pants, screaming 'Where *are* my car keys? WHERE ARE THEY?'

I'm sorry if you're a boy and you're reading this about my mum in her bra and pants, but honestly – why are *you* reading

my diary? My diary is a girl thing. Go buy

David Beckham's diary or something.

Anyway, Mum ought to know better.

She would tell me off for shouting.

I wanted to say:

'Where do you *think* they are?' – but

I didn't because she was really off on one.

Turns out her car keys were in the

fridge. We only found
them when Ollie
went to get half a
chicken and a loaf of
bread as a little
snack.

See? Weird! Keys in the fridge!

Then I asked Dad to explain to me how
plants take up water. (It was homework.
I mean, I didn't ask *out of interest!* I just
need to make that clear.)

He said:

'Not at the moment, Feely. I've got a lot
on my mind.'

Usually he would tell me about it and go on to tell me about every plant known to man and how they needed sun and where the sun was in the universe and if there might be plants on other planets and he'd just go on and on until my teeth bled and I begged him to stop.

Something was up with the parents.

I was getting a bit worried. Then there was another sign that something was coming apart. They started talking to each other!

Now, my parents *never* talk to each other. Oh they say things like 'Think I'll mow the lawn,' and 'You've got jam on your shirt,' and 'I'll take him — you pick him up,' but that's not *talking* — it's just saying stuff.

They don't talk about What Life Means or What is Wrong with the World Today.

Anyway, now they were talking (very, very quietly, almost as if they didn't want me to hear).

I went into the lounge and they were talking in there, but they went into the kitchen.

I went into the kitchen and they went upstairs into their bedroom. I went into their bedroom. ('Has anyone seen my sports shirt?'

'I told you – it's under Oliver's bed.')

They went and locked themselves in the bathroom. It was almost as if they didn't want me to hear.

This was serious! What was happening?

# Tuesday

Today at Drama Club I talked to Hannah

about it. We were waiting for the Drama

cupboard to be opened.

It turns out

the teacher forgot

about Drama Club

and went home.

He thought it

was Wednesday.

See what I mean about grown-ups?

Totally useless!

And I just love Drama Club! I'm really

good at drama. Pretending to be another

person is great. I really get into it.

I do acting in front of my mirror at

home. And I sing into my hairbrush.

I have to be careful Ollie doesn't hear me though.

Drama and Music are the best bits at school.

Anyway, when I stopped talking, Hannah said at once,

'Feely, – duh – they're getting a divorce!'

Of course! They were stressed. They were talking to each other. Those are the signs. Why didn't I think of that? It was staring me in the face. I was going to be the child of a broken home!

But what would happen to me? And Oliver. But mainly: me, me, ME!

Now Hannah is a divorce expert. Nearly everybody in her family is divorced or split up (she said 'splitting up' is like divorce but cheaper).

So many of her grown-ups are divorced that there are about thirty odd of them. Her dad is on his third wife and all of them had husbands before, and then all the husbands got married again.

Some of her brothers and sisters are old

enough to get married (and divorced) themselves.

They all seem to like each other (except Auntie Sophie and Uncle Ben, she said, but then they're still married) and they go on holiday to Tenerife together. They took up a whole plane last year.

Hannah has a charty thing her dad made her, so she can see who is 'proper family'.

This stuff was
really helpful.

'What does it mean
for me, Hannah?' (And
Oliver, of course, but
mainly me.)

'Well. You get loads of presents. I think
it's because all the grown-ups want you to
be happy, but as well I think they want you
to love them. They feel a bit bad about the
whole thing.'

OK that was good: loads of presents.

'And you get a choice of places to stay.
I stay at Dad's every other weekend and
Mum's on the other weekends, except when

I stay with Auntie Sophie who was Dad's first wife because she really likes me.

Aunt Bette cuts my hair and Uncle Lou who used to be married to Aunt Sophie does my nails. I'm sorted really.'

I could see why she needed a charty thing.

It sounded wonderful! Loads of grown ups to wash your eggy sports shirts!

'They do bang on a lot about horrible things they say their husbands or wives have done to them, but I just don't listen.'

Well that was OK, I already didn't listen to my parents.

'And are they happy? Are your grown-ups OK?' I asked.

'Oh yes, mine are OK, but they are all bonkers.'

Again ... so were mine. They would be OK.

# Wednesday

The more I thought about it, the more worried I got. My parents didn't *seem* happy. They seemed to be very *unhappy*. They didn't seem to be themselves.

In the end, I went and told Oliver. I thought he would laugh at me, but he had noticed they were acting weird too:

'Mum cooked me cheese on toast last night and took it out before the fire alarm went off.

'Dad told me the offside rule in one sentence instead of banging on about it until I was old enough to leave home. You are right, Feely. We need a family meeting!'

Now I put that bit in because I wanted it to sound as if we are the sort of family who has family meetings. Like those families on TV in America who all have perfect teeth. It sounds cool to be like that.

But we are not like that at all. We never have family meetings. If we feel strongly about something, we yell at each other (usually two or three people yelling at the same time) wherever we are (we're usually in different rooms, which is why yelling helps).

Oliver shut me out of the house once and I shouted at him through the letterbox

for half an hour, until old Mr Watkins next
door said I was making the dogs howl and
made Ollie let me in.

So there we were, all sitting round the table
in the dining room, looking like a normal
family and ready for our first ever family
meeting.

Dad said,

'What are we now — American?'

Oliver said quite loudly:

'I am fed up with this! Just for once we are going to talk to each other. Feely — tell them!'

So I told them about Hannah and all her brothers and sisters and the charty thing and Uncle Lou who did her nails and having two birthday parties and the every other weekend thing and how it was OK to tell us about Their Divorce.

There was a long silence. Then Mum and Dad laughed a lot. Dad did that snorting thing.

..... QUIET ....→

*It's not funny,* I thought. I was getting a bit hacked off to be honest.

'Oh, Feely,' Mum said, 'we're not getting a divorce. We're going to have another baby! I want to have another little baby just like you!'

What was I? A Pokemon card? Was she starting a collection of Feelys?

'Thanks a bunch!' said Oliver.

'Or like you, Oliver!'

'You can't have one like both of us!' Oliver was getting mad. He had a point.

I felt really happy though – it was not

the D word! The only thing was: would
I have to share my stuff with Future Brat?
Or, even worse, my bedroom? No way!

'Anyway – a sweet little baby,' said
Mum.

'Or not. We haven't
decided yet,' said Dad.
He went a bit red.

OK, so this was a
'Maybe Baby'! Then
they started arguing
and then they were shouting and I stopped
feeling happy.

I thought, 'Perhaps they *will* get a
divorce.'

I felt sad. Mum and Dad couldn't cope without each other. I know this for certain – they can't even cope together!

# Thursday
 # & Friday

It's been quiet at home for two days.

Nobody is talking to anybody else.

Everybody isn't talking to anybody.

Everybody is talking to nobody. You know what I mean. Everybody is in a mega strop!

Except me, of course.

# Saturday

## The Baby Experiment

In a week of strange things, this was this strangest! Oliver had a good idea.

No – I must be fair: a *great* idea. One of the world's greatest ideas ever.

He said we had to stop stropping around. He said we had to do something to 'move on'. He's a bit like Mum sometimes.

He decided we should borrow a baby and do an experiment on it.

That sounded a bit as if we were going to cut it up or see what happened if we left it in a bottle of vinegar. No. Not that.

We are just going to see if we can look after a baby, as a family, for all of today – just to see what it's like. Then we are going to have another family meeting and talk about it all 'like grown-ups'.

Oliver is getting to be really bossy. Dear Diary – do you think it will go OK? I am going to keep a record.

baby

## 8.00

Mum's friend, Auntie Sara, brings her baby round. It's a bit early but Auntie Sara says he's been up since five o'clock.

He's fast asleep now. He comes with a
Range Rover-load of stuff that Sara loads
into our lounge and hall and kitchen.

(I'm stopping the 'Auntie' thing – she's
not my auntie – I just call her that to fool
her into buying me a Christmas present.)

Our house now looks like Mothercare.
There's so much stuff in the lounge that
we can't see the telly. I don't like it. ☹

There's loads of stuff all over the floor and it's hard not to tread on it.

## 8.03

Sara leaves ('Bye now!').

## 8.05

Baby starts crying. He goes a bit red in the face.

Then Mum goes a bit red in the face.

He just won't stop and it's doing my head in!

## 8.06

Mum runs round in
a circle shouting,

  'Where's his
bottle, where's his
bottle?'

  I run round in a
circle shouting,

  'I don't know! I don't know!'

## 8.07

Baby drinks bottle. All of a sudden it's lovely
and quiet. Then his bottom makes a
squelchy noise as everything comes out the
other end.

## 8.08

Baby throws up down
Mum's back. I learn a
new bad word.

I thought I knew
all of them! I wonder
if there are any more?

## 8.10

Mum runs round in a circle shouting,

'Where's his nappies? Where's his nappies?'

Dad walks past and tells us all

about what is in baby poop.

Mum throws rattle at him

and misses.

Baby has nappy changed. Smelly or what?

## 8.15

Baby is just in the new nappy and he makes the squelchy noise again. Phew! That is a horrible smell. It made my eyes water.

It was quite interesting though. It wasn't like real poo, it was all yellow.

## 8.20

Baby watches Spongebob Squarepants. The

minute it finishes, he starts yelling again. I can feel a pain starting at the back of my head.

We watch Spongebob again — the same one! Then again! And again!

Well, you get the idea. I can tell you now, after a day of it, babies are no fun at all They just poo, drink and cry and then wee a bit. Maybe with the odd puke just to liven things up.

Oliver says they keep it up all night as well. They give a twenty-four hour service.

*How did Oliver help with this?* I hear you ask. Well, Diary, he got up,

found his skateboard,

went to the fridge

and then left

the house.

Other really exciting bits of the day:

Dad got his T-shirt caught in the baby buggy trying to put it up and had to be cut free. He also got a finger caught in it and made a big fuss because we hadn't got any elastoplast.

Then Mum left the baby outside the post office and had to run all the way back to fetch him, shouting,

'Oh no, oh no, oh no!' all the way.

Dad changed Baby's nappy because Mum was in a state after losing him and then Baby peed right into Dad's eye.

That was awesome!

Nearly best bit of day:

Sara put all the stuff back into the Range Rover and drove away.

Best bit of the day:

She came back for the baby.

It was so quiet after he had gone even

I still had a sort of ringing noise in my ears

from the noise he made.

The silence was wonderful.

All that was left was that wonderful

baby smell: poo, damp and sick.

# Sunday

We all sat down to our family meeting just as if we were in America. We were all sitting in silence. It was lovely. I love silence!

I never knew this, but you can hear silence.

QUIET

Then Mum said:

'I just can't do it! You forget what it's like! Perhaps we should get a dog instead.'

Can't do it.

Dad said:

'Dogs howl and you have to pick up their mess. A rabbit? They do nice little poos. It's made up of ... '

Oliver butted in before Dad could give us The Rabbit Poo Speech.

'Hamster?'

'Stick insect?' I said. 'Or a pet rock?'

I thought we couldn't kill a stick insect and they make no noise at all.

So we got a stick insect instead of another person and we were all fine with it.

I hope the stick insect ('Sticky') is going to be able to get out of his glass tank, go into the back garden, cut some leaves and shut himself back in, or soon he's just going to be a stick.

Ollie and I actually saw Mum kissing Dad in

the kitchen yesterday.
Ollie put his fingers in
his mouth, made a
noise like he was
making himself
sick and said,

'Get a room!'

So I guess everything's back to normal

## About the author

Barbara Catchpole was a teacher for thirty years and enjoyed every minute. She has three sons of her own who were always perfectly behaved and never gave her a second of worry.

Barbara also tells lies.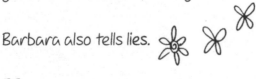

# How many have you read?

# How many
# have you read?

# Have you met **PIG**?

Meet P.I.G – Peter Ian Green, although everybody calls him PIG for short. PIG lives with his mum.

He is small for his age, but says his mum is huge for hers. She is a single mum, but PIG says she looks more like a double mum or even a treble mum.

PIG and the Ice-cream Cake
Barbara Catchpole

PIG Skives off School
Barbara Catchpole

PIG is a Blue Baboon's Bottom
Barbara Catchpole

PIG SuperPig!
Barbara Catchpole

PIG and the Baldy Cat
Barbara Catchpole

PIG Leaves Home (for a bit)
Barbara Catchpole

PIG Whopping Great Fib
Barbara Catchpole

PIG is Harry Snotter
Barbara Catchpole

PIG and the Rainbow Hair
Barbara Catchpole

PIG and the Big Quiz
Barbara Catchpole

PIG Gets Angry
Barbara Catchpole

PIG's Season's Finale
Barbara Catchpole